Poetry

To Frieda, David & Carol

from

Colin McAllister

December 2020

Poetry

ISBN: 978-178456-757-6
Perfect Bound

First published 2020 by UPFRONT PUBLISHING
Peterborough, England.

An environmentally friendly book printed and bound in England
by www.printondemand-worldwide.com

CONTENTS

Travel

Politics

Covid-19

St Andrews

Miscellaneous

Religious

Travel

ISLAND SKY

I must go down to the seas again, to the lonely sea and the sky
And all I ask is to embark again on the good ship *Island Sky.*
For this is a ship where the food is good and the wine flows
      free
And there is no other ship on which I would rather be.

I must go down to the seas again, for the call of a marine cruise
Is a call to visit new places along with lots of booze,
And all I ask is new friends to meet and new stories to hear
And good times to have shared when journey's end is near.

I must go down to the seas again, while my body still has life,
There to sail away from life's travail and all its trouble and
      strife,
And all I ask is good shipmates and laughter and lots of fun
And good memories to take home when the cruise is finally
      done.

Sonnet

THE AMBER ROOM

Each day our tour guide says, "Welcome, dear guests"
Who come to visit us from the West.
My name is Tatiana, I'm your guide.
I'll show you St Petersburg, far and wide.

We're going to visit Catherine the Great's palace,
The front of which she changed and spoiled. Alas!
The main treasure is the room of amber,
A place with its own special timbre."

Amber is said to help keep people healthy,
But to buy it you need to be wealthy.
"Now early to bed, early to rise
Makes a man healthy, wealthy and wise".

The man that buys amber, that man is wise,
He can buy it as he is early to rise.

AGEN-DA

OCTOBER 2019

I want to write a verbal litany
Of all I saw in Occitanie.
There is no lack of names that end in –ac,
Or bars where you can drink an Armagnac.

Of all the places to which I have gone,
There is none better than Carcassonne!
Surrounded by many an ancient wall,
This is a place that holds me in its thrall.

There are many cathedrals you can see,
But few there are that can equal Albi.
This cathedral has not one choir but two,
And its "Last Judgment" you simply must view.

There is a priory in La Romieu
From whose tower there is a splendid view.
This town was once infested with rats,
But it was saved by its domestic cats.

Which of the places on the pilgrim route
Is the prettiest? It's a point quite moot!
Among all the castles built by men,
Only a few can surpass Turenne.

We went to many places on our tour,
But the pearl of them all was Rocamodour.
This beautiful mediaeval village
Has long been a place of pilgrimage.

It seems that in France every road leads
To another of its old bastides.
I've seen so many that I've stopped counting,
But they are all on top of some mountain.

The villages along the river Lot
Are little jewels that time has forgot.
Saint-Cyr Lapopie stands above the rest,
By its tumbling heights my eyes are impressed.

There are places we went that did not rhyme,
That I will tell you of someother time.
This our journey started in Agen.
Now that we're back, I'll put down my pen.

Politics

Sonnet

THE SCOTTISH QUESTION

The Unionists and the Scottish Nats
Are forever having their little spats.
I wish they would give each other respect,
Before our country is completely wrecked.

Independence will come but with a cost,
Yet the bigger picture must not be lost.
Freedom lets a people hear its own voice,
And enables it to make its own choice.

The Union is not to be deplored,
Provided Scotland's views are not ignored.
With larger size come economies of scale –
But competing demands we must dovetail.

The only satisfactory solution
Is to have a federal constitution.

THE POLITICALLY CORRECT

"When *I* use a word", Humpty Dumpty said in a rather
scornful tone, "it means just what I choose it to mean – neither
more nor less", "The question is", said Alice, "whether you *can*
make words mean so many different things."

The people who have the greatest defect
Are those who are politically correct.
The PC brigade are for tolerance
Of their views, but others get no sufferance.

People no longer have sex, but gender –
All to suit a political agenda.
Climate change becomes climate disasters –
At twisting words they are past masters.

There are those who want "to save the planet".
What they don't like, they tax it or ban it.
The Greens want economic suicide,
Water-melons, green but all red inside.

Words and their meaning we must respect,
Let's end the politically correct!

Sonnet

VIRTUE-SIGNALLING

I am a roving virtue-signalman.
I practise virtue whenever I can,
I'm really into all this greenery –
Who cares if windfarms spoil the scenery?

The use of coal, oil and gas we must ban
With virtue-signals we'll be in the van!
Don't even mention the use of fracking!
This technique must never have our backing!

But what, you ask, if the wind does not blow?
Well, we'll just turn the heating down right low,
Or use some other energy channels
Such as the sun's heat through solar panels.

The real question that has to be weighed –
Warming, is it secular or man-made?

Sonnet

BREXITIS

I am suffering from Brexitis –
It is like a long lasting bronchitis.
We are in a crisis and it is chronic
And this has left me quite catatonic.

The debate between Leave and Remain
Has anaesthetised my weary brain.
I say this without hesitation –
Put an end to prevarication!

The nation's in total disunion –
Norway Plus, or a customs union?
The EU are playing us all for fools –
Just leave and follow WTO rules!

This disease has only one antidote –
There must be another People's vote!

Sonnet

ELECTION DAY 2019

Today is General Election Day.
The outcome is too close to call they say.
But I fear whichever way that it goes,
That it will not be the end of our woes.

Boris Johnson is a complete liar
And we will still be in a Brexit mire.
A Corbyn government would be much worse,
As it would soon bankrupt the public purse.

Corbyn being propped up by SNP
Is not something that I would like to see.
The LibDems stand on the side of Remain.
They'd put Brexit to the people again.

Which way the vote will go I do not know,
But it is a chilly wind that will blow.

Sonnet

US PRESIDENTIAL ELECTION 2020

A vote for Trump is great insanity,
Four more years of total inanity.
He thinks he's made America great again.
The rest of the world thinks him quite insane.

The political depths he has reached
Are the reasons he should have been impeached.
Those who, to find him guilty, were loath,
Have quite clearly foresworn their judicial oath.

US democracy is now broken,
Its outward façade is just a token.
Whether Republican or Democrat,
The President must be a plutocrat.

The Constitution must be amended
And gerrymandering be upended.

Sonnet

TRUMP v BIDEN 2020

As the poll figures begin to widen
Between President Trump and Joe Biden,
All good men and true must be very glad
To see the ousting of Donald the Mad.

Let us hope Americans have the sense
To reject Donald Trump and Michael Pence.
It is past time this serial liar
Faced an electoral funeral pyre.

Donald Trump is a MAGAlomaniac,
For him power is an aphrodisiac.
He thinks he is America's saviour
And that this justifies his behaviour.

The American people have a choice to make –
Their choice will the USA make or break.

Sonnet

TRUMP THAT!

About Donald Trump my best guess is
That he'll soon face the voters' nemesis.
No matter how loudly that he does boast,
He's going to be electoral toast.

There's nothing can give his ratings a boost,
As his chlorinated chicken comes to roost.
If American voters have the nous,
They'll eject this liar from the White House.

America's motto's "In God We Trust",
All men are mortal, and all men are dust.
So don't trust Trump, for he is just a crook
And the voters need to bring him to the book.

How to make America great again?
Vote for Joe Biden, and remove Trump's stain.

Sonnet

POTUS

Donald Trump is the man they call POTUS.
He doesn't have the brains of a lotus.
He thinks covid-virus we can settle
By injecting or drinking of Dettol.

This childish fool who thinks he is so smart,
This chat-show host who thinks he stands apart,
Who will make America great again,
Is in fact America's greatest bane.

Smarter by far is an orang-utan
Than this self-promoting charlatan.
He is a know-all who knows but nothing,
With instant knowledge made up on the wing.

America, don't vote him in again!
This man is crazy, and he is insane!

Sonnet

THE OVAL OFFICE

In the Oval Office sits the POTUS.
He was elevated there by OTIS.
He says "Don't worry about this virus.
The US is great, the world admires us."

"The land of the brave, the land of the free,
Has nothing to fear, just you wait and see.
All we need is ultra-violet light,
A swig of Dettol, and we'll be alright."

"This epidemic is all China's fault
And so all trade with them we must now halt.
We must stay in splendid isolation.
No trade means no bugs, that's our salvation."

"Vote for me and every card is a trump!
Vote for Joe Biden, you vote for a chump!"

Covid 19

Sonnet

COVID-19

Those people who've been called Co-vidiots
Are like the Border sheep named Cheviots.
They think the virus will not infect them,
But their selfishness will not protect them.

And those who set off a buying panic
Indulge themselves in actions quite manic.
There's enough food to meet everyone's need,
But not enough to meet these people's greed.

All these unsocial actions we now must cease,
If we're to control the spread of this disease.
Otherwise this virus will overwhelm
The brave staff at the NHS's helm.

Only by acting sensibly *en masse*
Can we be quite sure that this too will pass.

Sonnet

LOCKDOWN

As we are all urged to self-isolate,
The streets of our town are quite desolate.
It's as if everyone were on the Moon.
I hope this lockdown will end soon.

"No man is an island" was never more true –
Lack of human contact makes me so blue.
I feel as if I'm Robinson Crusoe,
Marooned on a desert island of woe.

Who can now say in all sobriety,
"There is no such thing as society".
One thing none of us should ever forget
Is that we are all in each other's debt.

When we shall have come through this terrible mess,
We should thank our wonderful NHS.

SOME ENCHANTED EVENING

Some enchanted evening, you may see a stranger
Across an empty room,
And somehow you know, even then, she is a danger
And could well be your doom.
To save your existence, keep to a safe distance.
So don't you get too close, you must just let her go,
Or you will regret it for all of your short life.
You can say it with flowers that you love her so.
When this is over, you can make her your wife.

NHS

O NHS! O NHS!
With fulsome praise I
you address!
No matter if we're
young or old
You serve us all with
hearts of gold.
Your care and skill they
inspire us!
With your help we'll
beat this virus!

Sonnet

ALL IN THIS TOGETHER

It's said 'we are all in this together',
And this viral maelstrom we will weather.
Until we have built up herd resistance
We must keep to a safe social distance.

This new virus is so detrimental
To our health, both physical and mental.
It's the unseen enemy everywhere
Transmitted by our coughs through the air.

One of Four Horsemen of the Apocalypse,
Co-vid 19 is on everyone's lips.
Hugs and kisses we now must forbear
Until we get through this living nightmare.

This pandemic is a tremendous test,
But we'll defeat it if we do our best.

Sonnet

HYDROXYCHLOROQUINE

Donald Trump thinks hydroxychloroquine
Is the best drug that has ever been.
For those with malaria it's a cure,
For those with Covid it makes death more sure.

Stop Covid-19 by drinking some bleach
Is the nonsense this idiot does teach.
We should say this to this blood-sucking leech,
"Why don't you go and practise what you preach?"

This Trump is nothing but a mountebank
Undeserving of Presidential rank.
Everything he does is completely fake.
I wish he'd just go and jump in the lake!

This man needs to go to the funny farm,
Before he does us all any more harm.

Sonnet

DON'T PANIC!

If you have a virus that makes you feel queer,
Then you should go and drink *Corona* beer,
Or one that reaches parts others don't reach,
Or you could always go and drink some bleach.

If you are not in the finest of fettle,
I recommend you should drink some Dettol.
It kills 99% of all germs –
It's even good for intestinal worms!

Hydroxychloroquine is quite the best –
Just drink some and you'll be back at your best!
It cures malaria, so why not this?
No vaccine exists, it's all hit and miss!

Let's hope one day we will have a vaccine,
Until then we must wash and keep our hands clean.

Sonnet

VCV DAY

Millions of workers say, "Someone hire us,
We've been sacked by the coronavirus.
It's all very well being on furlough,
But we are all now running out of dough."

We must put an end to his recession
Before it becomes a Great Depression.
Even if it means a rise in the Debt,
A Budget deficit we will not reject.

Though the strain of lockdown we all abhor,
The health of the nation we must restore.
As slowly our freedom we regain,
We will feel it has been worth all the pain.

May memories of wartime inspire us
To work together to beat this virus.

St Andrews

Sonnet

ST ANDREWS UNIVERSITY

Anger mounts at the Uni's arrogance,
As the town fights back with all resistance.
Town and Gown relations are like a boil,
As the Uni's growth the town does spoil.

There has to be some *modus vivendi*,
If Town and Gown are to remain friendly.
The Uni's students must leave their bubble
And learn not to cause townsfolk trouble.

Students do not have to pay the Council Tax
And their behaviour is often lax.
So here is something of which to take note –
No taxation means they should have no vote.

The Uni is only part of the toun –
Forget this, and the toun will ding it doun.

Sonnet

ST ANDREWS DIVERSITY

Where once was St Andrews University
We now have the St Andrews Diversity.
By policy of dissimulation
Has come the Uni's accumulation.

Instead of promoting social cohesion,
The Uni fosters a great lesion,
As its own values on the town it does impose
And those of the townspeople it does oppose.

A Uni's home is in its community,
With which it should live in peace and unity,
But too often the Town and Gown are divided,
And each by the other is derided.

I don't think this tale will have a good end,
Unless the Uni does itself amend.

Sonnet

TOWN AND GOWN

Compare the Uni to a parasite
Which feasts on its host by day and by night,
So that now the Town has become the Gown
And locals in a sea of students drown.

Or consider it a cancerous growth,
Such that Town or Gown can live, but not both.
Student numbers should no longer increase
And the Uni's expansion must now cease.

The Uni must give the Town some respect
Or the Town will be completely wrecked.
Just now they are like a foreign body,
Rejected by almost everybody..

To live with the Town in peace and unity
Is to respect the wider community.

Sonnet

THE CRITICAL MASS

Now the Uni's achieved critical mass,
Lined up against it, the critics amass.
As the student waves roll to the town's shore,
Loud the seagulls cry "Enough and no more!"

Just like bees or wasps forming a swarm,
Or like birds in a field awaiting a storm,
Students have become something of a pest,
Despite their motto "Ever to be best".

The proper study of man is mankind,
So students should learn not to be so blind.
Students are like migratory birds,
Or like birds of passage in other words.

If students were like the nightingale's song,
They'd be more welcome and they would belong.

Sonnet

THE TOWN OF ST ANDREWS

St Andrews used to be a wondrous place,
But of that there now remains but a trace.
It was a place for townsfolk to enjoy,
Which now outsiders exploit and destroy.

I'm sure I'm not the only one who begs,
"Don't kill the goose that lays the golden eggs!"
Destroy not the town for commercial greed –
Respect others' space and what they need.

Town and Gown, will you keep this in focus –
Good neighbours remain in their own locus.
There is room enough for everyone's need,
But not to satisfy rapacious greed.

Dum Spiro Spero is the motto of the town,
But short-sighted selfishness will ding it down.

Miscellaneous

Sonnet

A GOOD WIFE

Is there anything better in this life
Than to have a loving and loyal wife,
Who helps a man to live a better life,
And who is never trouble or strife?

But what if your wife is a total nag
And to your progress is a total drag,
And if her garrulous tongue you cannot gag,
Then I must pity you – oh what a hag!

But as around the dance floor you birl,
Consider that a wife is a great pearl.
So do not be forever a selfish churl,
But let the winds of love your sails unfurl.

A good wife (or a man) is hard to find.
I hope you find one even though love is blind.

RUDOLPH THE RED-NOSED REINDEER

Rudolph the red-nosed reindeer
Had a very shiny nose.
Rudolph liked to have a beer,
So he got a beery nose.
Once he turned out all queer –
He'd drunk too much Atholl Brose!
Rudolph had no reindeer dame,
Since he liked to have a drink.
Only himself he had to blame –
That's what all the reindeer think.
Rudolph, don't be such a lush –
Please bring us some Christmas cheer,
Driving through the frozen slush,
Bringing in a Good New Year.

BAD KING WENCESLAS

Bad King Wenceslas oft went out
For to do some reivin'.
Tho' he suffered from the gout,
That stopped not his thievin'.

He stole when the moon was bright.
Cattle and sheep he took.
He stole everything in sight –
He was a royal crook!

"No need for you to shiver,
Just because there's some snow.
Stand you here and deliver
And I will let you go."

This tale has no happy end,
'Cos a reindeer gored the king.
It was Rudolph, Santa's friend.
Serves him right for stealing!

IN PRAISE OF CHEESE

Without chocolate I can live with ease,
But one thing I can't do without is cheese.
Cheese is the perfect complement to wine
And I want cheese ev'ry time I dine.

France is a land of many a cheese
And each and ev'ry one my taste buds please.
From mighty Roquefort to Camembert
French cheese will grace any bill of fare.

If Gruyere is not your cup of tea,
Then cut yourself a piece of creamy Brie!
From The Netherlands comes Leerdammer,
Enjoyed by many an Amsterdammer.

The Netherlands' pride, Gouda and Edam,
Go well with a panini of ham,
And the Spanish cheese that's called Manchego
With a slice of quince will go toe to toe.

One of England's great poets was Milton
And its greatest cheese has to be Stilton.
Now here's a cheese which can tell its own tale –
It comes from Yorkshire, it's called Wensleydale.

The cheese that is known as Caerphilly
Is eaten by Welshmen willy-nilly.
While Scots think a cheeseboard rather dowdy,
Unless it contains some oatmeal Crowdie.

Germany produces Cambizola,
Not half as smelly as Gorgonzola!
Also from Italy comes Parmesan –
Of all its cheeses it is in the van.

There is such a variety of cheese,
That it is not hard to find one to please.
Cheese is better than chocolate by a mile!
There is always a cheese to make you smile!

Sonnet

WHERE?

I was once in the middle of nowhere
And then I thought I must be somewhere,
And that somewhere could be anywhere.
Now were I in the middle of nowhere,
I could just as easily be somewhere,
Or I could equally be anywhere.

Now if nowhere has a middle,
Then it poses us a riddle –
It must be that nowhere has its bounds,
And this is not as odd as it sounds.
The answer to which my mind is tending –
A middle must start and have an ending.

If I am nowhere, then nowhere is here,
And if I am somewhere, then here is there.

EDINBURGH ZOO

There's an elephant in Edinburgh Zoo
Which creates piles and piles of smelly poo
That's nothing compared to the kangaroo
Which swears so badly that the air turns blue.

There's a hippo which thinks it's quite hip,
And in a mudbath takes a daily dip.
In the next pool is a crocodile,
And they have been friends for quite a while.

Next door to them is an armadillo
Which keeps itself clean by brushing with Brillo.
Its neighbour is a female anteater.
It is quite friendly – I think you should meet her.

Across the path is a Russian meercat.
His name is Sergei – well fancy that!
Right next to him there is an old groundhog
Which passes the time by writing his blog.

Then there is a European lynx –
Shy, inscrutable – who knows what it thinks?
In the next pen are three guanacos
Which feed only on Mexican tacos.

From Madagascar comes a lemur –
How long it's been there I am not quite sure.
It lives next door to a female baboon –
The noise it makes can be heard on the moon!

There's also an Australian dingo,
But no one can understand its lingo.
It's next door to an Aussie wombat.
They fight each other in daily combat.

Lying out in the sun are some iguanas
Gorging on their favourite bananas.
Next door to them are two testy tapirs.
They're prone to take offence and the vapours.

There are some ostriches so lofty,
Which carry themselves with an air quite haughty.
They think the other inmates are riff-raff,
But they have to look up to the giraffe.

There is also an elegant gazelle.
It runs so fast and it is such a swell.
To survive it has to win ev'ry race,
As it needs its predators to outpace.

There are also African blue parrots.
They dine daily on nothing but carrots.
Their neighbour is an ancient wise vulture,
Which thinks it alone has any culture.

Other inmates are too many to name,
But among them are some really big game.
Here ends my list of *Animals Who's Who.*
When you are in Auld Reekie, go to the zoo!

SEVEN LIMERICKS

There was a young lady from Portree
Who used to go drinking on a spree,
But too much whisky
Made her quite frisky,
And she ended up thinking she was the bee's knee.

There was a young lady from Lochee
Who used to like to swim in the sea,
One day the ebb tide took her out
And not a person heard her shout
And that was the end of the lady from Dundee.

There was a young lady from Istanbul
Whose glass was not half empty, but half full.
As she staggered around from bar to bar
She had admirers from near and from far.
She told them all their chat up lines were just a load of old bull.

There was a a young lady from Madrid
Who loved to dine on fried squid.
She was dressed all in pink
When one squirted its ink
She complained that really had put on it the tin lid!

There was a young lady from New Guinea
Whom everyone thought was a bit skinny.
No matter what she ate
She did not put on weight,
So her doctor prescribed her zucchini washed down with lots
    of Martini.

There was a young lady from Vanuatu
Whose back sported an elaborate tattoo.
This splendid scene
Was seldom seen
Because to show it was considered completely and utterly
    taboo.

If you want to greet a green-backed turtle,
Then tap its back with a porridge spurtle.
You may hit it on the doup
But just don't say "turtle soup"
Or from you away with speed it will hurtle.

Sonnet

NOTRE DAME DE PARIS

Notre Dame de Paris, you me inspire
And I am devastated by your fire.
You represent the heart and soul of France!
On the Ile de la Cite is your stance.

A great rose window your nave adorns
And in you is kept the Crown of Thorns.
Great historical events you have seen,
Including the marriage of Scotland's queen.

Notre Dame, you are France's joy and pride!
Despite the fire, hope for you has not died.
I hope before long you will be restored.
The loss of you mankind cannot afford.

Notre Dame de Paris, I wait the day
When once more to you I may come to pray.

Sonnet

ENGLISH PRONUNCIATION

What is it about the English and their R's?
This shibboleth their language mars.
R's in unwelcome places they intrude
And R's where they should be found they exclude.

If you wish to be called to the Bar,
Then first you must learn to misplace the R.
Unless you want to be dragged through the mud,
You must always address the judge as M'lud.

The Scots pronounce their R's because they roll them.
Those who do not, the Scots cannot thole them.
The best English is found in Inverness,
Spoken clearly, and with a Gaelic stress.

To speak good English you must learn to parse,
So you can tell your elbow from your ****.

Religious

Sonnet

DID YOU LOVE ENOUGH?

The road of life can be rambling and rough
And more than once one can lose the way,
But what matters at the end of the day
Is this, 'did you love, and did you love enough?'

Often with pride one's own self-worth does puff –
That great vanity can undo a man –
As he considers himself in the van
And forgets to ask did he love enough?

Now love of self only itself does buff
And others it considers not at all,
Except to be at its beck and call.
True love asks did I love enough?'

At life's end this will be the final test –
Did you love yourself, or did you love the rest?

Sonnet

THE WAITING ROOM

I have now arrived in Heaven's waiting room,
Where Death awaits to take me into his womb.
My bags are packed and I'm ready to go.
I hope God his Mercy to me will show.

Now that I'm in life's departure hall
I await with Faith and Hope the Lord's call.
I hope my soul's lamp with grace is lit
And that I'll not go to the fearsome pit.

Lord, on your great Mercy I rely,
For my past sins I cannot deny.
O, grant me the grace of true repentance
And so through Heaven's gate gain my entrance.

O Lord, you are my hope and great stay.
After my death may I rise to your Day.

Sonnet

THE WORD OF GOD

O Gardener of my soul, thin is the soil
That You do till; and it is full of weeds.
My enemy planted them; him do foil.
Rain on my soul those graces which it needs.

Melt with your great love the stones in my heart,
Then remove from it each and ev'ry weed.
Uproot the worldly thorns that keep me apart
And plough my heart to receive your Word's seed.

Let not earthly pleasures me distract.
May my furrow be completely straight,
And let not my soul with guilt be racked.
Then let me enter through the narrow gate.

Now having sown your Word in my heart's field,
May it then produce a plentiful yield.

Sonnet

FAITH, HOPE AND CHARITY

Faith is the key that opens Heaven's door
And by Faith the unseen God we adore.
Our faith is based on Jesus Christ Our Lord –
No word is truer than that of the Word.

Thanks to Hope we need not fear or cower,
Because of God's mercy and his power.
During our lives we often fall and fail.
Our hope is that God's love will prevail.

The greatest virtue is Charity,
By which we try to live in amity.
Charity covers a whole range of sins
And this is the virtue that Heaven wins.

Faith, Hope, Charity are a trinity
And the greatest of these is Charity.

Sonnet

HEAVEN

The beginning of Heaven is love on Earth.
We are made for love from the day of our birth.
To live is to love, and to love is to live,
With all the love that the human heart can give.

To love God is to love one's fellow man,
Not holding back, but with all that one can.
"This is the command I give to you –
Love one another, as I have loved you".

Our love is shown less in words than in deeds.
This is the love that to Heaven proceeds.
It is the perfect love that casts out fear,
And brings Heaven's Kingdom to us so near.

Love your God with all your heart, soul and mind
And in Heaven your name in gold will be signed.

Sonnet

DEBIT AND CREDIT

Every time you sin you use your SINcard,
So you should always be on your guard.
Each good deed is marked on your credit card
And will have its heavenly reward.

So take good care how you spend your time!
If you want Heaven's mountain to climb
Don't live a life of sin and pleasure –
Each deed is rewarded in good measure.

Faith is the key that opens Heaven's door,
And by Faith the unseen God we adore.
Our faith is based on Jesus Christ Our Lord.
No word is truer than that of The Word.

Over the gate of Heaven above
There's written just one word and it is Love.

Sonnet

THE LAST DAY

Lord, let me not seek life's earthly plaudit,
But, rather, to pass the Heavenly audit.
May I acknowledge all my sins and blame
When I stand before You in all my shame.

Lord, without Your grace we can nothing do –
With Your grace my heart and soul renew.
Lord, show me Your paths and show me Your ways,
So that I may love You all of my days.

Lord, I know that I'm made of nothing but clay.
Teach me to love You and to obey.
I am weak and I am prone to stray.
Good Shepherd, bring me back to Your way.

On the Last Day, when I wake from death's sleep,
Place me, Lord, not with the goats, but with the sheep.

Sonnet

LIFE'S RACE

I do not wish to be someone of note,
Enough to be a history footnote.
When I shall have ended my life's race,
May I have left the world a better place.

Troubles in life we ahall not have to seek.
In face of these, we must learn to be meek.
Tempests and storms there are certain to be,
But Christ will calm them, as he calmed the sea.

I ask not freedom from trouble and strife,
But only the grace to live a good life.
The things of this world will crumble to dust.
Lord, in You alone will I place my trust.

When death calls me to encounter my fate.
Lord, grant me safe entrance through Heaven's gate.

Sonnet

LEAD ME LORD

Lord Jesus, whom I adore,
You have said "I am the door",
Open then that door to me
And let me your glory see.

Let me enter into your fold,
With your saints to be enrolled.
May I be one of your sheep,
Resting there in peace so deep.

Offence to You I have given,
May my sins now be forgiven.
Suffuse my soul with your grace,
So I may yet see your face.

O Lord, lead my soul to rest
In the Garden of the blest!

Sonnet

GOOD FRIDAY

Today I saw a man crucified
And I wondered at how well he died.
No curses nor bad words did he say,
Instead for all of us he did pray.

Before him two brigands we crucified,
We placed him between them on either side.
To one he promised that day Paradise,
At the other's fate we can only surmise.

His last words were that it is completed,
By which he meant sin had been defeated.
At his death an eclipse darkened the day,
As his spirit went up on Heaven's way.

My name's Longinus, the centurion.
I say, this man is truly God's scion.

Sonnet

HOLY SATURDAY

I, a disciple, woke this day with gloom,
Yesterday we placed Jesus in the tomb.
This has been a most dreadful Passover.
I cannot believe his life is over.

His death to me has been a total shock,
Smiting the Shepherd has scattered the flock.
We thought that Jesus was the Messiah,
But he was treated like a pariah.

My heart feels like it is a lump of lead.
I don't want to live if Jesus is dead.
With this grief and sorrow I cannot cope,
Yet he did not leave us bereft of hope.

These are the words that Jesus did say,
"**I** will die, but will rise on the third day."

Sonnet

EASTER SUNDAY

The sun had risen, the morning was clear,
As the women to Jesus' tomb drew near.
"But who for us will roll away the stone?
We're not strong enough to do it alone."

But the stone had been rolled during the night
And by the tomb stood an angel in white.
"He has risen as he said, he's not here.
Go and tell the others, and have no fear!"

To the apostles they ran with great speed,
"The Lord is risen, he's risen indeed!
Come quickly, and be no longer afraid.
Come and see the tomb where Jesus was laid."

"We heard his words with great jubilee,
'I go before you to Galilee'.

Sonnet

MARY MAGDALENE

"Sir, are you the gardener? Where's my Lord?"
"No, Mary, I'm risen, true to my word.
Go and tell my friends that they will me see,
Having preceded them to Galilee."

The heart of Mary was then filled with joy
And peace and contentment without alloy.
To the apostles she hastened to say,
"The Lord has risen, yes, this very day."

Mary, faithful to Jesus until death,
His rising has given to you new breath.
We pray, ask Jesus to deepen our faith,
So to reach Heaven suffering no skaith.

Mary, in bliss in Heaven above,
Teach us on earth better Jesus to love.

Sonnet

THE UPPER ROOM

The apostles met in the upper room,
Their minds were overwhelmed with dule and gloom.
Trauma and distress blocked out what Jesus said
All they could think of was that Jesus was dead.

What do we do and where do we go now?
Peter, you are our leader, show us how.
We live in fear of persecuting Jews.
Peter, tell us now what path we should choose.

He said that I would deny him thrice,
And this I did almost in a trice,
But he prayed that my faith would prevail,
So now in this hour I will not fail.

Today is only the second day,
So wait one day more, that's what I say.

Sonnet

DOUBTING THOMAS

Thomas, the Twin, was lacking in belief,
And so he spent a week on needless grief.
Then to the apostles appeared the Lord,
"Thomas, why did you not believe my word?"

See here my hands and see here my feet.
Now you've seen them may your faith be complete.
Thomas, now put your hand in my side.
I am alive, I am the one who died.

"My Lord and My God" is what Thomas said,
"You are my God, You are the Living Bread,
You are my Lord, and You are my Saviour,
The Chosen One, on whom rests God's favour."

"Thomas, you believe because you have seen,
Blest are those who believe, not having seen."

Sonnet

THE HOLY SPIRIT

All Hail to You, great Paraclete!
Through You may our faith be complete.
You are the finger of God's right hand,
Against Your power none can withstand.

You who are sevenfold in Your grace,
Through You may we see the Father's face,
And through You also the Eternal Son,
Who by His death Heaven for us has won.

Holy Spirit, who came at Pentecost,
Breathe new life into a world that is lost.
You came upon us like tongues of fire:
Renew us and with love our hearts inspire!

On Jesus You descended like a dove:
Now inflame in us the fire of Your love.

BV - #0011 - 171220 - C0 - 197/132/4 - PB - 9781784567576 - Gloss Lamination